Reincarnation

LIANA BROOKS

OTHER WORKS

ALL I WANT FOR CHRISTMAS

All I Want For Christmas Is A Reaper
All I Want For Christmas Is A Werewolf

FLEET OF MALIK

Bodies In Motion
Change of Momentum

HEROES AND VILLAINS

Even Villains Fall In Love
Even Villains Go To The Movies
Even Villains Have Interns
Even Villains Play The Hero (books 1 – 3 omnibus)
The Polar Terror

TIME AND SHADOWS

The Day Before
Convergence Point
Decoherence

SHORTER WORKS

Fey Lights
Prime Sensations
Darkness and Good

Find other works by the author at
www.lianabrooks.com

Reincarnation

INKLET #90

LIANA BROOKS

Inkprint PRESS
www.inkprintpress.com

Print ISBN: 978-1-922434-20-3
eBook ISBN: 9798201261559

www.inkprintpress.com

National Library of Australia Cataloguing-in-Publication Data
Brooks, Liana 1982 –
Reincarnation
38 p.
ISBN: 978-1-922434-20-3
Inkprint Press, Canberra, Australia
1. Fiction—Fantasy—Historical 2. Fiction—Short Stories

First Print Edition: September 2022
Cover photo © Andrej Podobedov via Pixabay
Cover design © Inkprint Press
Interior art © Amy Laurens

REINCARNATION

I DIDN'T BELIEVE IN REINCARNATION. That turned out to be a problem, standing there in the equivalent of a celestial waiting room arguing with someone who had a softly glowing white tablet, who'd met me at the moment of my death and started talking about what came next.

Within minutes there were three men arguing with me, all white-haired and slightly round. A woman with soft gray hair and a white hanbok that Jung Kyung-hee would have killed for explained it was okay I didn't believe in reincarnation, I was going back to Earth anyway.

Being dead, I didn't need to breathe, but I took a breath anyway. Habit, more than anything. And I tried to see the bright side: space travel, the cure for migraines...

Maybe this time I wouldn't get a broken body. Or maybe I'd be reincarnated so far in the future I wouldn't need to worry about that at all.

LOL.

Turns out reincarnation isn't linear. Or sensible. Or anything that appealed to me. The growing group of elderly souls planning my return trip were gathered around a map, pointing and talking excitedly about a country I'd never even heard of that existed thousands of years before I was born.

Apparently the country needed saving. And after fifteen thousand attempts, no soul born into the body of the nation's hero had actually become the national hero.

It was like going back to be Mu Lan, except at least I'd heard of China and knew vaguely what Mu Lan needed to do. I didn't have a clue about this other place. Never heard of it.

Didn't know the language.

Didn't know how to swing a sword, fire an arrow, or do anything else.

I tried to explain!

It was definitely cultural appropriation, right? I didn't have any ancestors from... wherever this place was. I hadn't studied it, except for maybe three paragraphs in an AP History book when I was fifteen.

I'd lived a good life! Why did I need to go back? What did I need to learn?

That was the point, they told me. I *had* lived a good life. Helped lots of people. Done good things. Left the world better than I found it. If I could do it once, I could do it again! Just... sweep in and fix history.

I tried reasoning with them. If I didn't know the language, how was I supposed to do anything? Were they giving me any hints? A cheat code? Magic? Something?

They told me I'd pick it up as I went along. Learn the language like a native.

I was almost out the door before I realized what that meant: Like a native? They meant LIKE A BABY!

I was going to have to do everything over again from step one! Learn to walk, talk, eat, everything. In a world with no penicillin and probably brutal laws (just guessing).

There was no way.

I tried arguing I should go to whatever hell was available instead.

It didn't work.

They kept going on about how things needed to be fixed. And I was so good at this. And look at what a nice life I'd already had! And wouldn't it be fun to try something new?

Besides, if it all went sideways again, it wasn't like I'd remember the life I'd just left.

All I needed to do was step through this suspiciously sparkly arch, just like that, very nice. Well done. Don't mind the little blue marble, that was a just a memory anyway. I wouldn't need that. Now, over to the glowing doorway. Very good. Don't worry. This won't hurt at all…

They hustled me out the door with no fanfare, and barely any worries.

In retrospect, that was also a mistake.

I did live a very good life last time. Excellent. Some might even say remarkable. But I'd picked up slight-of-hand out of boredom and the pickpocketing was really just to maintain my memory and keep my arthritic hands active. And, seeing as how I was already headed to another eternal reward, it didn't seem like anyone would, you know, care if my previous memories came along for the ride. Just this once.

Talk about awkward.

I was a demisexual in my last life and having to suck a stranger's tit for nourishment for nine months was terribly awkward. I was not born to be sapphic (sorry, girls). And the cradle was in the main living space. It was not fun. Not being able to remember those early years is a blessing I missed.

As soon as I could, I started talking. Full sentences. In what I considered one of my native languages.

My new parents said I spoke the Divine Language, which wasn't true at all. What I spoke was three languages in a trench coat that shook down other languages for verbs and participles.

I'd been semi-fluent in a number of languages in my past life, and none of them would be invented for thousands of years.

So there I was, babbling away, living in a daub hut with a straw roof trying to figure out what disaster I was supposed to save everyone from. Starvation? Plague? Volcano? Wild animals?

Childhood is terrifying enough *without* knowing about dysentery and the millions of ways you can die on the Oregon Trail. But I knew. I knew a lot of very generalized concerns, but nothing specific.

So, once I got a handle on the local language and became the youngest orator in the history of this very small valley, I went to work.

Put the midden a long way from the well.

Wash your hands.

Invent the toothbrush.

Basic cow pox vaccines (thank you

strange Kdrama I watched with a fever one week, I can't wait to see you invented again).

Sterile clothes.

Therapy.

So much therapy.

Village life is more stressful than it looks.

I could diagnose anemia by looking at eyes and gums. I splinted broken legs (way to go 6th grade survival teacher at that one weird mountain camp! I learned something!).

I picked up archery, sword fighting, and the habit of leaving emojis on every form of writing in the hope that it would go viral on Twitter and my past-future-self would at least read a couple more paragraphs. By my mid-teens, nothing had worked, but I kept trying.

We took up trade negotiations with a neighboring village. We established treaties. I learned a couple more dialects to pass the time. When a plague broke out, I taught people about masks, quarantine, and how to build a catapult to send the neighbors food. Social distancing was a thing and—somewhere—Egypt was getting ready to build some pyramids.

I told all the neighbors that was going to be lit, but the literal translation makes Egypt sound way hotter than it actually was... Is? ...Will be?

By my twenties I figured out why they took memories away.

I missed my best friend. She wouldn't be born for three, maybe four thousand years. And I couldn't call her on the telephone even if she was here because I didn't have a telephone, and I didn't know how to make one. Or electricity. Or a satellite system. Or any tech, actually.

A terrible, terrible life choice. Next time I will make sure to dedicate some free time to researching solar cells and how to build them in any environment. We could settle the moon a lot faster if we got around to space travel before Catholics were invented.

Oh, also, slight time travel tip... Since it doesn't matter, just smile and nod at any religion that comes along. It's better than the alternatives.

So, where was I? My late twenties maybe? At this point everyone was pressuring me to have kids, which...

Haha hahaha! I did that in my past/future life and I know what it's like without drugs. The idea of doing it in a mud hut was not appealing to me.

But you know, I was keeping my eyes open. In case someone changed my mind. After all, I needed someone to honor my last wish and bury me with a dagger. One round of reincarnation was enough.

Next time I'm going through that detention center *armed*.

I'd gone for a ride and was circling back to a dust up where some of our local boys and some strangers were fighting.

And then I saw him. The man I'd loved a lifetime ago. Those soft brown eyes I'd seen at a bus stop just before heading to college.

I must have sounded mad, screaming in multiple languages for them to stop, to not hurt him. They'd almost killed him. But I knew him. I knew those eyes. He'd come and found me.

I told him I'd missed him so much. That I loved him. How had he found me?

He didn't understand a word.

None of his memories of our last life together were there. But it didn't matter. If I was going to save this nation from disaster, the least they owed me was another lifetime with my soulmate.

It was wonderful.

We had long lives.

We did have kids... eventually.

We were so happy.

He left earlier than I did, but I'd told him to wait for me up there. And I taught him how to pick pockets and speak a little of the languages I remembered. He died with his head in my lap as I told him about the life ahead of us, and he promised to wait at the bus stop for me.

Now I'm old and gray. My eyesight is fading. I keep a dagger on me, for death could come at any time.

But I never found the disaster I was supposed to stop. The great tragedy I was sent to avert never arrived.

Nothing I did was that large. Like my last life, my actions were small things. I raised no armies. Led no battles. Waged no wars.

There had never been a great adventure for me. Only the small things that fill every life. I helped the sick. Fed the hungry. Listened to the ones who wanted to talk. Sat in silence with those who needed a friend.

As death comes, I hope it was enough. I hope I lived this life well. I hope, somehow, I did what needed to be done to save these people from their terrible fate.

Thousands came before me to live this life, to save these people, but—selfishly—I hope I'm the last. I hope no one else takes my spot to live a life with the one I loved, with my bemused parents, with my beloved children, with my dear friends. I hope I did enough.

I hope I was enough.

THE MAKING OF *REINCARNATION*

There are so many small things we do every day that we don't consider heroic or extraordinary. Get up, feed the kids, get everyone to work and school, walk the dog, say hello to a neighbor, answer a question online, call a friend, make some dinner, give some cash to a panhandler…

Most people will never see the end result of all their interactions. How the little things like bringing a friend dinner or having a kind word for someone in the hall might change the direction of their life.

Heroism isn't always going on a great adventure to slay an evil overlord; sometimes it's about making a vaccine, negotiating peace, or making sure there's enough food on the table for everyone to go to bed with a full belly. The quiet lives of thousands of unsung heroes have done more to change the world than any war. Wars draw lines, but to heal from those scars, you need generations of people willing to forgive, accept, and embrace people who were once an enemy.

Read more by Liana Brooks!

EVEN VILLAINS FALL IN LOVE

CHAPTER ONE

I knew from the first time I saw my wife that I wanted her naked. Of course, seven minutes later I wanted revenge. It wasn't that she had handed me my first defeat or ruined my chances for world domination that year, it was the way she kissed me good-bye. She sent my head spinning, then walked away as if I were the least important person in the world.

Once my arm healed, I stole some new equipment, cloned some new minions, and I felt a little different.

I wanted revenge, with a side order of naked.

ACROSS THE DINNER table, Tabitha devoured him with dark, ocean-blue eyes. She put a bite of lettuce in her mouth, full lips pursing around it. Eating salad never looked so good. Her tongue darted out to lick away a stray drop of dressing. She winked at him, promising with every move to do the same to him. "It's almost bedtime," she said, her voice husky and luscious.

"I don't wanna go to bed!" one of the quads screamed.

"What about cake? Don't we get birthday cake?" another asked.

Evan winked back at his wife from the far side of the table, separated by a few feet and four precocious just-turned-five-year olds, all as stunning as their mother with big, round eyes and hair that fell in loose curls meant to trap hairbrushes and sticky substances.

He had to peek at the eyes to see who was talking. Maria had green eyes, Angela's eyes were blue like Tabitha's, Delilah's eyes were brown like his, and Blessing—their stillborn who miraculously survived—had purple eyes. The waif in question had blue eyes.

"Angela," Evan said, "after dinner it's pajama time, and then story time."

"Mommy doesn't have a bedtime!" Angela wailed.

Tabitha winked at him again. "Tell you what, tonight Mommy will go to bed the same time you do. Right after we eat cake." She leaned over to give Angela a hug.

All Evan could see was the deep V plunge of her tight blue shirt. Oh, yeah. Crime didn't always pay, but altering someone's moral compass sure put the O's back in the bedroom.

The cake was split into fourths, equal parts purple, white, green, and blue so each girl could have her favorite color in the cake.

Baking four cakes was unreasonable; there weren't any grandparents left to celebrate with, and neighbors had an annoying habit of asking uncomfortable questions. Saying little things like, "You look just like Doctor Charm! Do you remember him? Whatever happened to that guy? Do you know how hard it is to put together a good Villains vs. Heroes fantasy league without him?" made for awkward evenings.

So they had a quiet family party. Cake, then presents, after which he hurried the girls off to bed so he could read Dilly Duck's ABCs in record time before rushing to the bedroom, hoping to catch Tabitha still in the shower.

She was already out and wearing a blue satin robe that caressed her skin in exactly the way he wanted to. Rose-scented candles cast sensuous shadows on the walls.

Tabitha turned, lips curved in an inviting smile. Long fingers twined with the sash of her robe. She tossed her honey-blonde hair in the way she always did when she was about to argue, posing with feet apart and one hand casually resting on her waist. "Sweetie, we need to talk."

Evan wiped grease-stained hands on his jeans as he forced a smile. "Sure, babes, anything you want."

"Really?" She slunk forward, all sinewy limbs and doe eyes. "Promise?" Tabitha nuzzled his nose. One hand flirted up the back of his neck to play with his hair. The other traveled downward, right to his zipper.

Oh, yes, the little Morality Machine in the basement was working just fine. Another thirty, maybe forty years of this and he'd consider retiring.

Or turning the machine down so his wife wasn't quite a sex kitten every day of the week.

Maybe only days with Y in them.

"Sweetie?" She nibbled his ear. "I want to go back to work."

"What?" Evan actually pushed himself away from her, something he wasn't sure was possible in any other circumstance.

Tabitha tucked her chin and pouted.

"Tabby-cat, I love you, but work? I've got my... stuff... in the lab. I'm busy. And we can't afford daycare for the girls. We're barely making ends meet as it is. Do you really want to go back to being Zephyr Girl? Crime fighting is a game for the young, baby. You're not nineteen anymore."

"I'm twenty-nine. A very"—her hips pressed against his tight jeans just so—"very healthy twenty-nine."

He shivered at her touch. "You're cheating."

"I want to do this, Evan." She ground against the thick denim.

"You can do me all you want, baby."

She stepped back, frowning. "I'm serious."

"So am I." Evan sighed, reaching for his wife. "Sweetie, I love you, but what's the point in being a superhero?

The government stipend barely covers the dry-cleaning bill. If it's money you want, write another tell-all superhero book. The Spanish Mask sold his third last month."

Tabitha crossed her arms. "I don't want to write another book just for royalties while you're between jobs."

He waved a finger at her. "I'm not between jobs. I work freelance in the computer business. I'm self-employed. That's not the same as being between jobs."

"Between paychecks then."

"We will have a solid income. This project I'm working on, Tabby-cat, it's going to set us up for life. We're never going to worry about money again. I promise. Give me a couple of weeks and everything is going to be perfect." He caught her hand and pulled her into his arms. The faint scent of her spicy perfume left him dizzy with need.

She rested her head on his chest. "I

want to save the world. Have you seen the news, Evan? An entire town in Kansas held hostage for a week by a bomb scare before a superhero was able to get in to defuse the situation. A week! I could have that done between grocery shopping and paying the bills. Ten minutes, no pulling punches."

"I know, baby. No one is better at this stuff than you. But I need you at home, Tabby. Having you out there scares me. I'm terrified I'd lose you. Why don't you wait until I finish this project? I'll be done by the time the election rolls around. Two more weeks. Once I get paid we'll look at this again. I have that armor design for you, I just need some time to put it together."

Tabitha sighed. "You've been saying that since we got married."

"Well, my nights are busy." He nibbled her ear as he tugged her sash loose. "Are you complaining?"

Tabitha stretched against him, sending a delightful frisson of lust up his spine. "I thought you gave up the super villain schemes."

He twitched. "I did, baby. Of course I did."

"But you're keeping me here. Isn't that a little selfish? Just a teeny-tiny bit super villain-ish?" She slipped her hand between his pants and his skin.

"Ah!" He caught her hand so he could think clearly. "Not selfish. Necessary. Like oxygen or sex."

"Don't you mean water?"

"No, definitely sex." Evan slid her robe off and tossed it into a corner. "Come here, Tabby-cat, I'll make you purr."

She tugged at his shirt, pulling it up. The shirt joined the robe on the other side of the room. "What are you doing down in that lab?" she asked as her hands drew lazy circles on his back.

Ten seconds, that's all he'd need to

get her panties off. Three more to drop his pants. "What was the question?"

"What are you doing in the lab? What's this project?"

"Oh, computer stuff. I told you. To help tally everything on election night. I'm trying to make the process run smoother so we don't have to worry about recounts."

"Hmmm." She gave him a dubious frown.

Tabitha was built like a supermodel and had a superhero name straight from Campy Comics, but her brain was Mensa all the way. "And this computer program has nothing to do with world domination, or get-rich-quick schemes?"

Evan contrived to look wounded. "Tabby-cat, how can you ask that?"

"Because you spent ten years as a villainous criminal mastermind?"

"I wasn't a mastermind, I was a super villain, there's a difference. Masterminds are just thugs with money. My crimes had artistic flare. I was practically Robin Hood! Robbing from the rich and scandalous, and giving to me.”

“Robin Hood gave to the poor,” Tabitha said with a laugh. “You were never poor.”

He caught her hand, pulling her close. “Poor is relative. Besides, I’m reformed now. You showed me the error of my wicked ways. Although”—he leaned in for a kiss—“if you’d like to remind me why I gave up a lucrative life of crime, I have the evening free.”

Keep reading! Head to
www.inkprintpress.com/
lianabrooks/heroesandvillains
/love/
to buy your copy now!

ABOUT THE AUTHOR

LIANA BROOKS is definitely not a traveler from another life, complete with memories intact. That's definitely not where she gets her story ideas from… Why do you ask?

She writes science fiction in every form, from sprawling space operas romances (the *Fleet of Malik* series, starting with *Bodies In Motion*), to the antics of a super-powered family (the *Heroes and Villains* series, which can be read in any order), to intricate time-travel murder mysteries (the *Time And Shadow* series, starting with *The Day Before*).

Liana also maintains a soft spot for paranormal romances. She writes the popular *All I Want For Christmas* novellas. You can learn more about her and her books at www.LianaBrooks.com.

INKLETS

Collect them all! Released on the 1st and 15th of each month.

Dancer, Dreamer
Seer
LIANA BROOKS

As Time
Whirls Slowly
Past
AMY LAURENS

Far More
Satisfying
Than Hell
AMY LAURENS

Just
Another Day
In Hell
LIANA BROOKS

Moon AND
Morning
AMY LAURENS

Some
Impropriety
Expected
AMY LAURENS

NEON SNOW
LIANA BROOKS

Reincarnation
LIANA BROOKS

More Than
Mushrooms
AMY LAURENS

DOUBLE ISSUE
INKLET #093
How To Make A Star
& The World Ended
LIANA BROOKS

INKLET #093
CAUGHT
IN THE ACT
AMY LAURENS

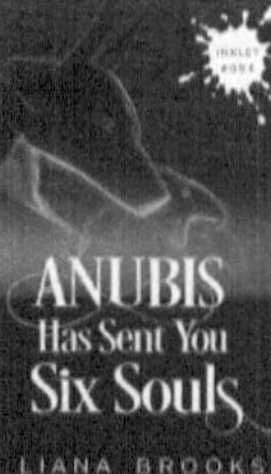

INKLET #094
ANUBIS
Has Sent You
Six Souls
LIANA BROOKS

INKLET #095
PRAYER TO A
GODDESS
LIANA BROOKS

INKLET #096
Love In The
Time Of Corona
AMY LAURENS

INKLET #097
RECRUITMENT
AMY LAURENS

INKLET #098
IDENTITY
Theft 101
LIANA BROOKS

INKLET #099
Curses
With Benefits
AMY LAURENS

INKLET #100
NECROMANCER
TROUBLES
LIANA BROOKS